THIS WALKER BOOK BELONGS TO:

____

____

____

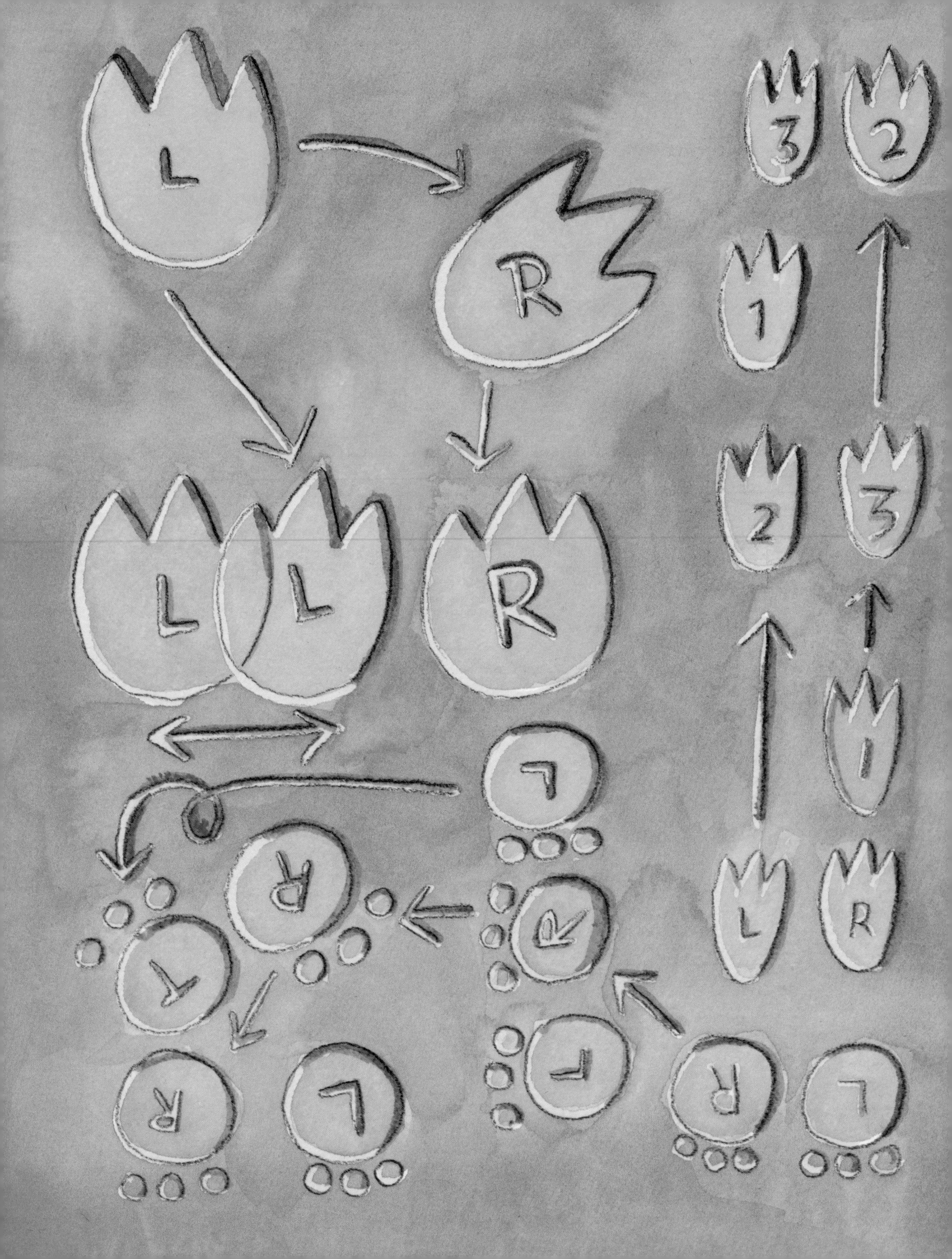
L
R
L
L
R
3
2
1
2
3
1
L
R

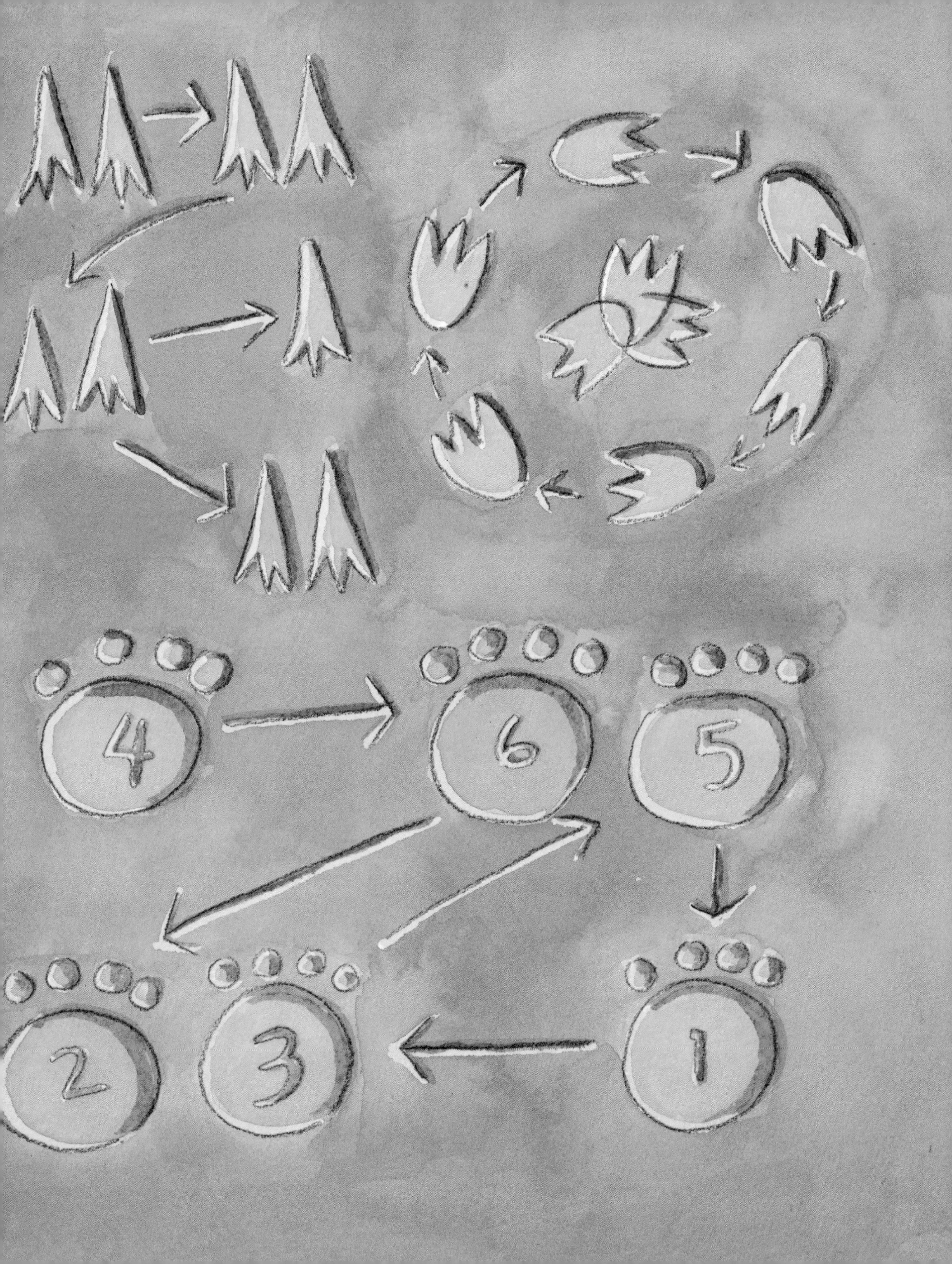
4
6
5
2
3
1

For Alex and Sam, with love
– C. D. S.

To Sarah, Timmy, Allison, Charlie and Nancy
– S. N.

First published 1997 by Walker Books Ltd
87 Vauxhall Walk, London SE11 5HJ

This edition published 1999

11 13 15 14 12

This book has been typeset in Cafeteria Bold

Printed in China

British Library Cataloguing in Publication Data:
a catalogue record for this book is
available from the British Library

ISBN 978-0-7445-6345-0

www.walkerbooks.co.uk

Carol Diggory Shields

illustrated by Scott Nash

Word went out 'cross the prehistoric slime:
"Hey, dinosaurs, it's rock 'n' roll time!
Slick back your scales and get ready to romp

On Saturday night at the **Dinosaur Stomp!"**

By the lava beds and the tar pit shore,
On the mountain-top and the rainforest floor,

Dinosaurs scrubbed their necks and nails.
They brushed their teeth and curled their tails.

Then – ready, steady, go – they trampled and tromped,

Making dinosaur tracks for the Dinosaur Stomp.

Plesiosaurus paddled up with a splash

Protoceratops ambled along with her eggs.

A batch of bouncing babies followed Mama Maiasaur.

A pterodactyl family flew in for the bash.

Diplodocus plodded by on big fat legs.

The last time she counted, she had twenty-four.

The old ones gathered in a gossiping bunch,
Sitting and sipping sweet Swampwater Punch.

Dinosaurs giggled and shuffled and stared,
Ready to party, but a little bit scared.

Then Iguanodon shouted, "One, *two*, **three!**"
Started up the band by waving a tree.

Brachio-, Super-, and Ultrasaurus
Sang, "Doo-bop-a-loo-bop," all in a chorus.
Ankylosaurus drummed on his hard-shelled back,
Boomalacka boomalacka! Whack! **Whack!** **Whack!**

Pentaceratops stood up to perform
And blasted a tune on his favourite horn.

They played in rhythm, they sang in rhyme,
Dinosaur music in dinosaur time!

Duckbill thought he'd take a chance:
Asked Allosaurus if she'd like to dance.

Tarchia winked at a stegosaur she liked.
They danced together, spike to spike.

The Triassic Twist and the Brontosaurus Bump,
The Raptor Rap and Jurassic Jump.

Tyrannosaurus Rex led a conga line.
Carnosaurs capered close behind.
They rocked and rolled, they twirled and tromped.
There never was a party like the **Dinosaur Stomp**.

The night-time sky began to glow.
Volcanoes put on a firework show.
The ground was rocking – it started to shake.
Those dinosaurs danced up the first earthquake!

The party went on – it was so outrageous,

They stayed up well past the late Cretaceous.

When the Cenozoic dawned they were half asleep.
They yawned big yawns and put up their feet.

And they're *still* asleep, snoring deep in the swamp.
But they'll be back ... next **Dinosaur Stomp!**

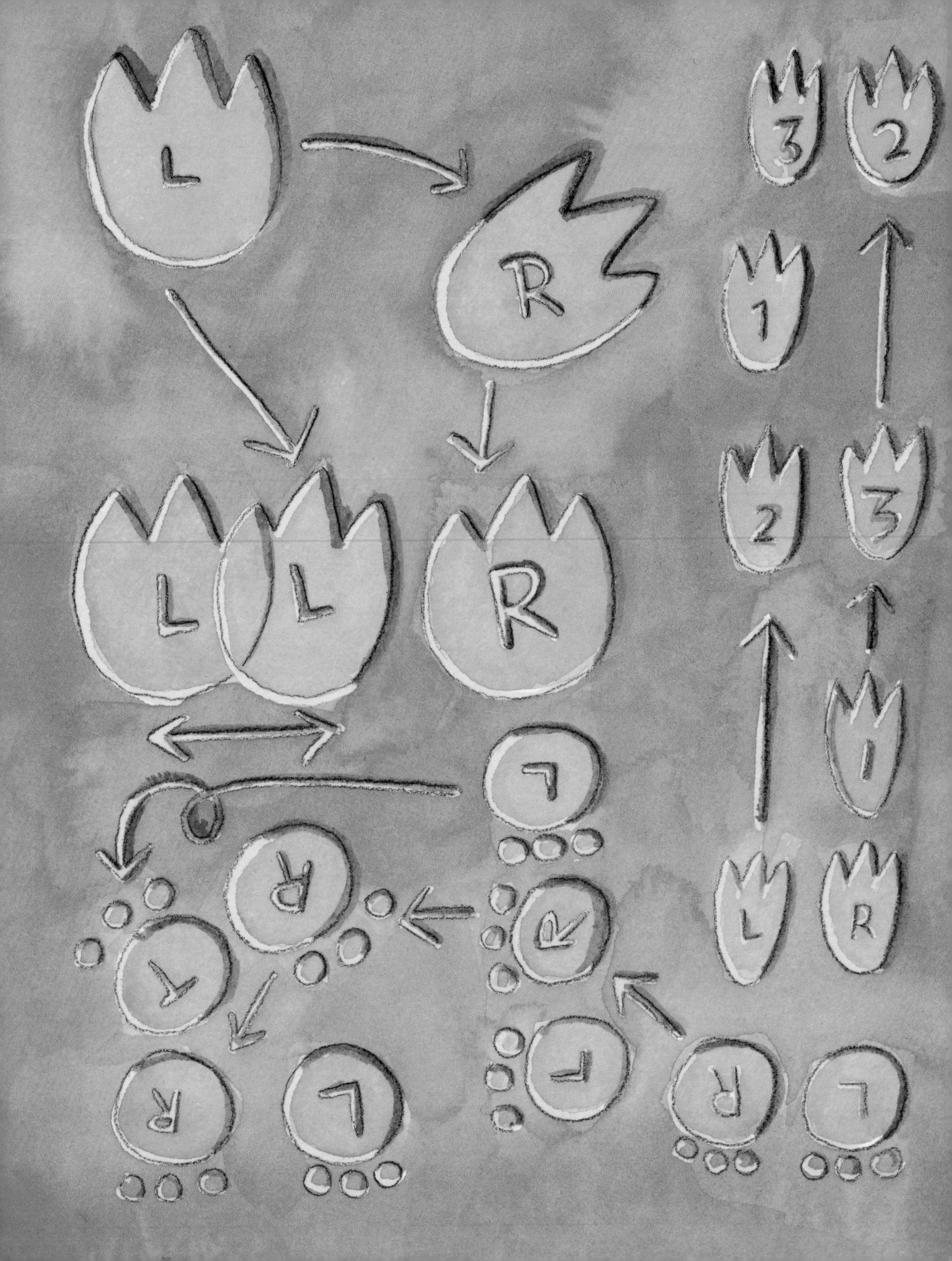
L
R
L
L
R
3
2
1
2
3
1
L
R

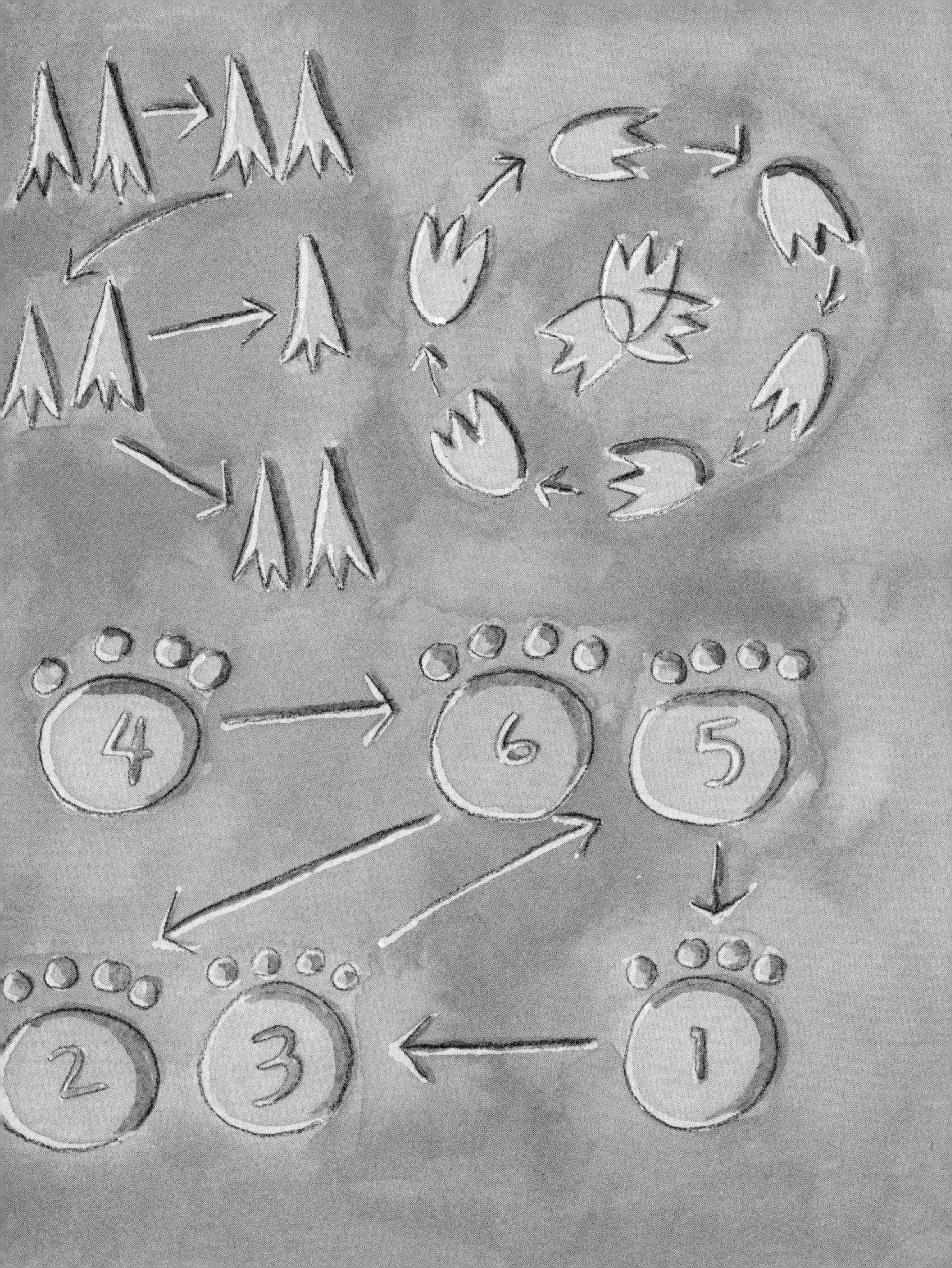
4
6
5
2
3
1

WALKER BOOKS is the world's leading
independent publisher of children's books.
Working with the best authors and illustrators
we create books for all ages, from babies
to teenagers – books your child will
grow up with and always remember. So...

FOR THE BEST CHILDREN'S BOOKS,
LOOK FOR THE BEAR